TwinFabulous!!
This book is dedicated
To my favorite Twins
Jordan & Jasmine.
I love you double time!

ISBN: 9798511614595
Imprint: Independently published

Published by: La'Tosha Price
Pricelessstorytime@gmail.com
Edited by: Carlos Price
Illustrated by: La'Tosha Price
tosharp@gmail.com

Introduction

I'm a creator, a visionary, a playwright, and a storyteller. I approach the world with the eyes of an artist, the ears of a musician, and the soul of a writer. I see the endless possibilities when others see only problems and obstacles. Musical plays, children's art museums, and my own children have been sources of inspiration to me, as well as gospel music and praise and worship. I value the importance of abandoning momentarily my adult wisdom and knowledge so that I can accurately tell a story about life through a child's eyes. I believe that quality is one of God's gifts to me.

Another of His gifts to me is writing. I love to write! Maybe that's because words flow easily from my brain to my fingertips, and my heart beats rapidly with excitement as my efforts allow an idea to become a reality on the paper in front of me. No matter the time of night or day that I sit to focus upon writing, once the story is inside me, I have to tell it! If my family members are nearby, they must hear about what I'm thinking. And then the magic happens when I assume the mind of a child and present my story in written form.

All children delight in reading stories about characters looking and acting like they do. However, for reasons of history, racism, economics and so much more, there are too few children's books where African American kids like mine get to feel validated by the content of the stories they read. I felt compelled to take action by using my gifts to honor God and children together. So, this book about a series of events in the life of "JoJo & Jazz'" details incidences that happen to all children, but the faces of all the characters here are of persons of color.

My goal is to spread the word about the power of accomplishing your dreams, and the excellence in reading that produces the power of knowledge! I learned to dream through reading, learned to create dreams through writing, and learned to develop dreamers through teaching. I shall always be a dreamer. Dreams really do come true, so I invite readers to come along and dream with me.

La'Tosha Price

Hey! My name is JoJo. This is my sister Jazz. We are Twins! We are a bundle of TwinFabulous fun, even if we share the same face!

We have a loving bi-racial family, and we love to take vacations all over the world with them. Our adventures are so TwinFabulous!

Would you like to join us on our family adventures? If so, first stop is Paris!

"Wow!" We're finally going on vacation," JoJo said to Jazz as they were packing their suitcases.

"Paris - here we come!" Jazz said happily.

"This is our first airplane ride!" exclaimed JoJo excitedly.

"It's our first time to Paris too," Jazz added.

"Look Jazz," JoJo said. "I even packed my satin scarf and little French hat for the trip!"

"This trip is going to be TwinFabulous!" the girls said at the same time.

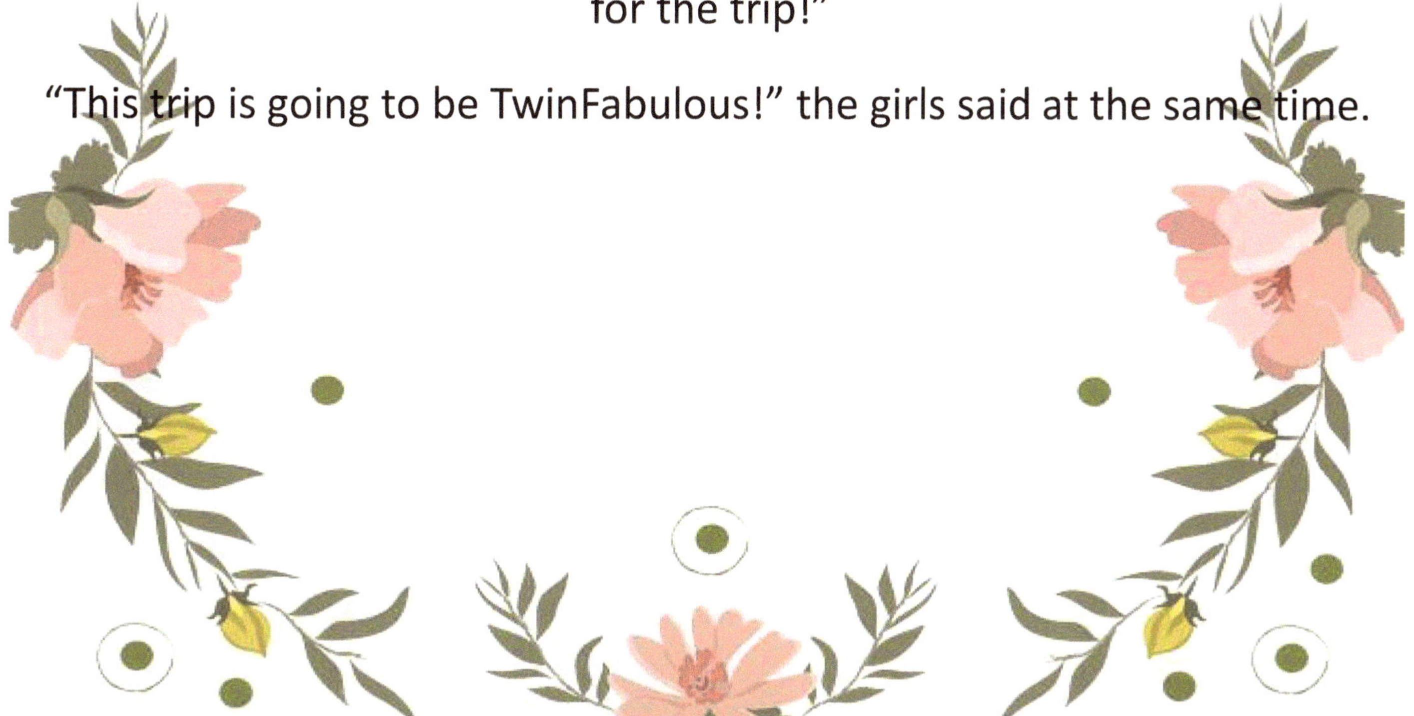

Today we are off to Paris France! Paris is commonly known as the "City of Light."

Paris did not receive the nickname "City of Lights" for the Eiffel Tower's twinkly lights, nor as a reference to the city's reputation for romance.

Paris is called this because it is the most lit city in the world!

At the check-in-counter, the ticket agent stamped JoJo's and then Jazz's tickets.

Daddy Reggie looked and looked for his, and finally found it stuck in Momma Paula's big traveling purse that she uses to pack snacks in.

The ticket agent stamps each ticket. "Now, don't lose this," she warned daddy.

Both girls giggled at the same time and turned to walk to their appointed gate.

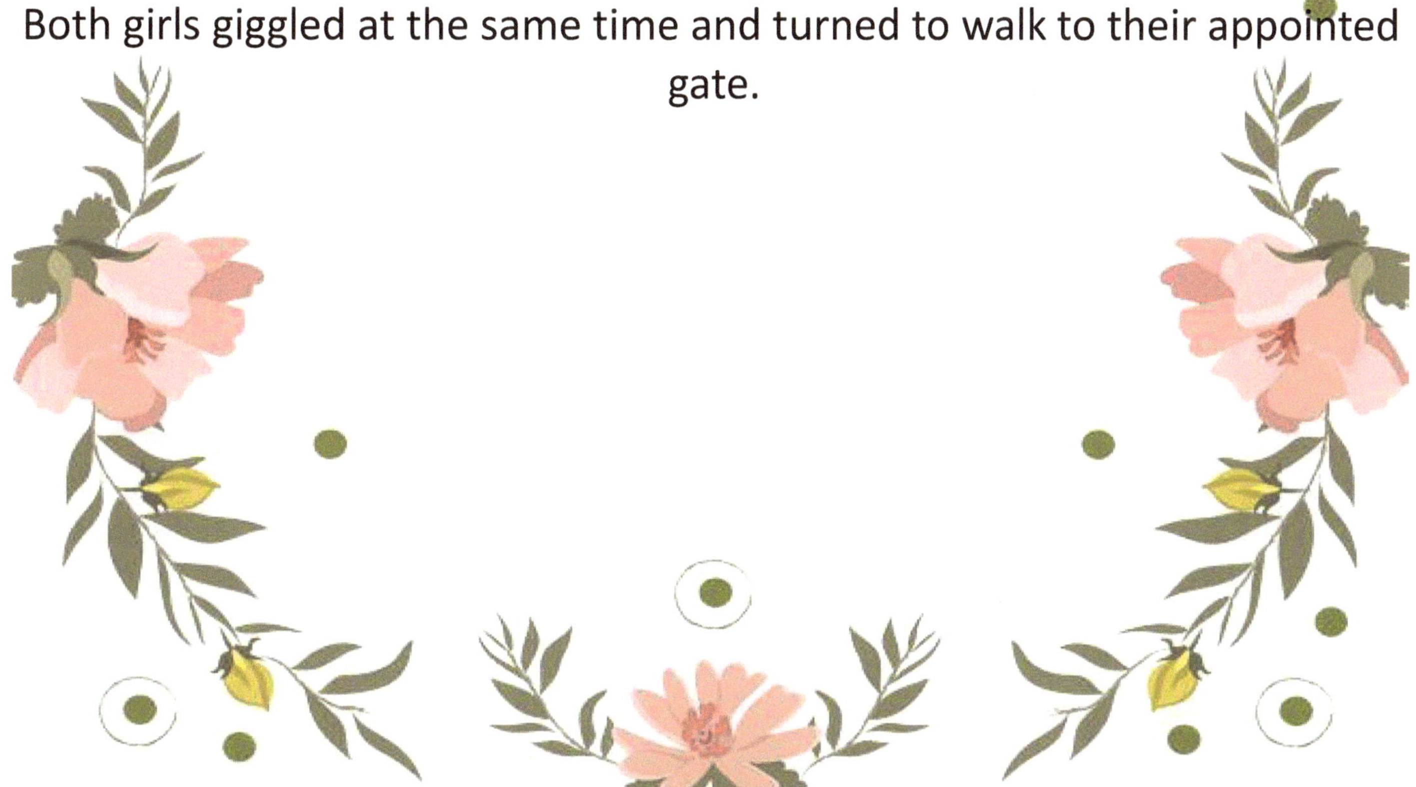

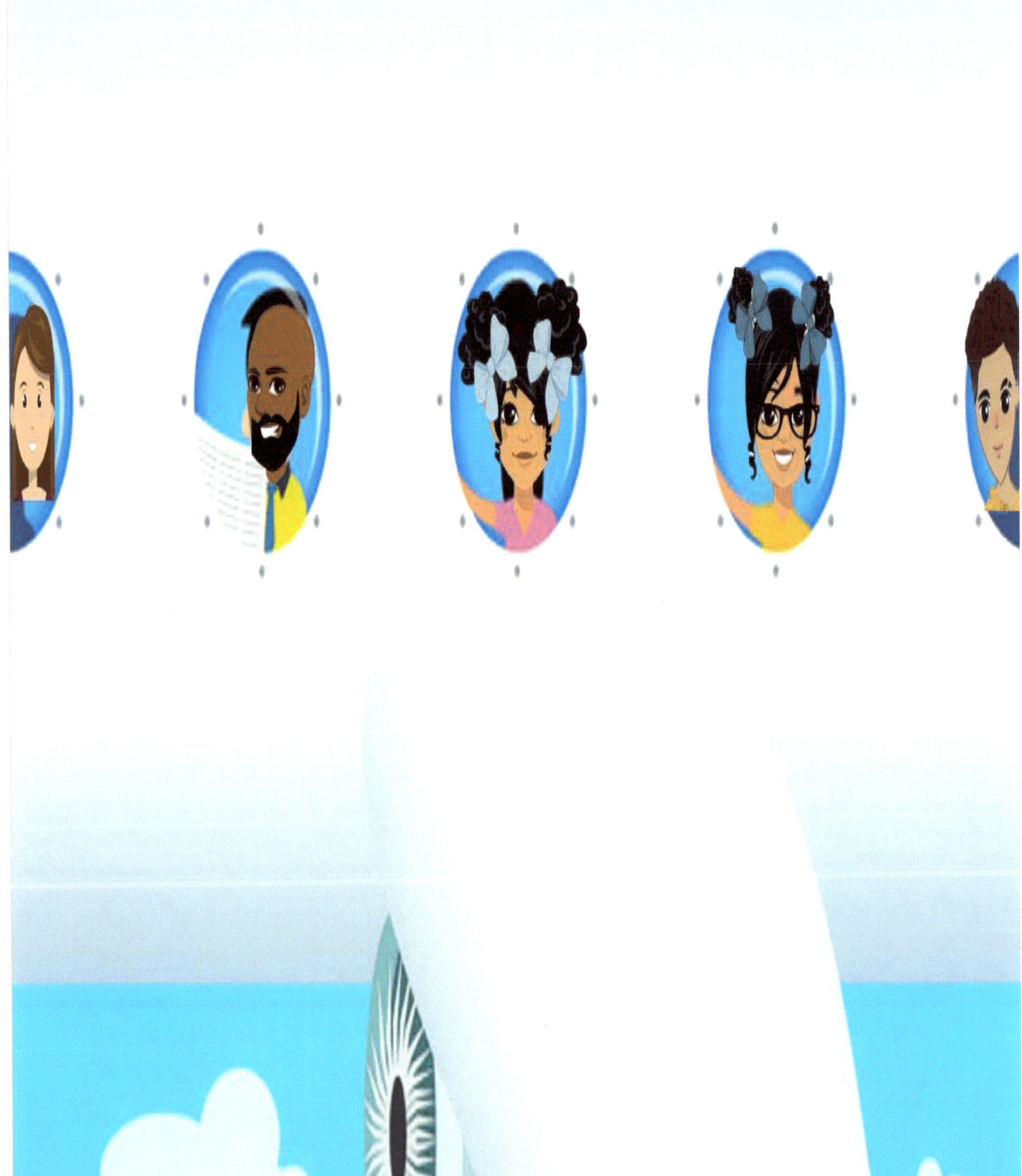

"Jazz did you know that the best time to visit **Paris** is from June to August and September to October?" JoJo asked.

Both summer and fall have its ups and downs. From June to August the weather in **Paris** is just about parfait (perfect).

Average highs are in the high 70s and there are long days of sunshine. JoJo continued to explain just as the flight landed.

First stop the Eiffel Tower!

"JoJo did you know that the **Tower** Has a Wife?" Jazz asked. "A Wife!" JoJo shouted. Erika "Aya" **Eiffel** (née Erika LaBrie), is an American **female** competitive archer and advocate. She famously **"married" the Eiffel Tower** in a commitment ceremony in 2007.

"Also, the size of the **tower** changes with the weather, and the tower was only meant to stand for 20 Years." Jazz explained. It was built as an entrance for the 1889 World's Fair and completed on March 31, 1889.

The **tower** was the world's tallest man-made structure for 41 years until the completion of the Chrysler Building in New York in 1930.

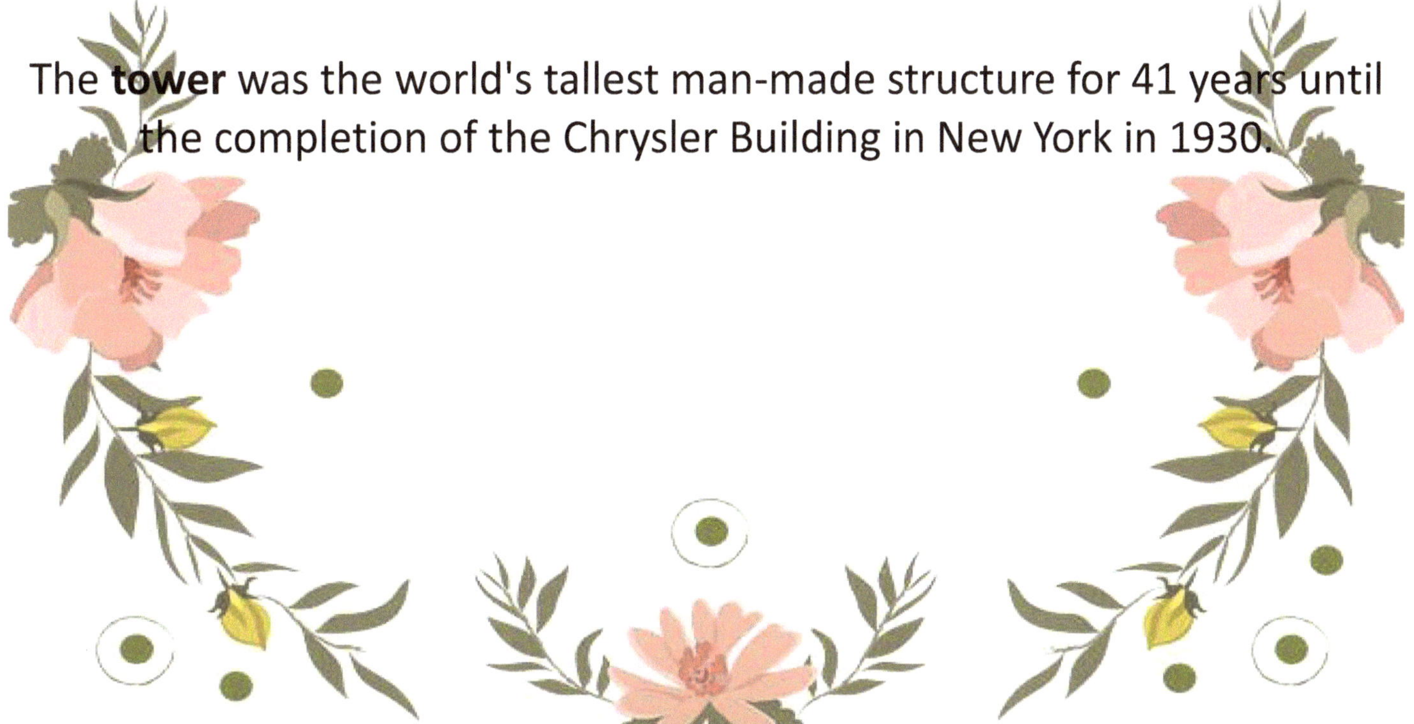

BAKERY
A tasty Treat Freshly Baked
OPEN
BREAD & DESSERTS
SALE
%

"Next stop La Maison d'Isabelle the place has the best croissant in Paris!
JoJo shouted.

"While we are here, let's practice some of our French." Jazz suggested.
"Like when the waitress came to take our order?" JoJo asked.

(Parlez-vous anglais?) Which means do you speak English?
The waitress replied, *"Non"* which means No. The girls placed their order
and enjoyed fresh Croissants and Tea.

Once they had finished, the girls told the waitress *"Merci beaucoup"* which means thank you very much.
Next Stop the Louvre Museum!

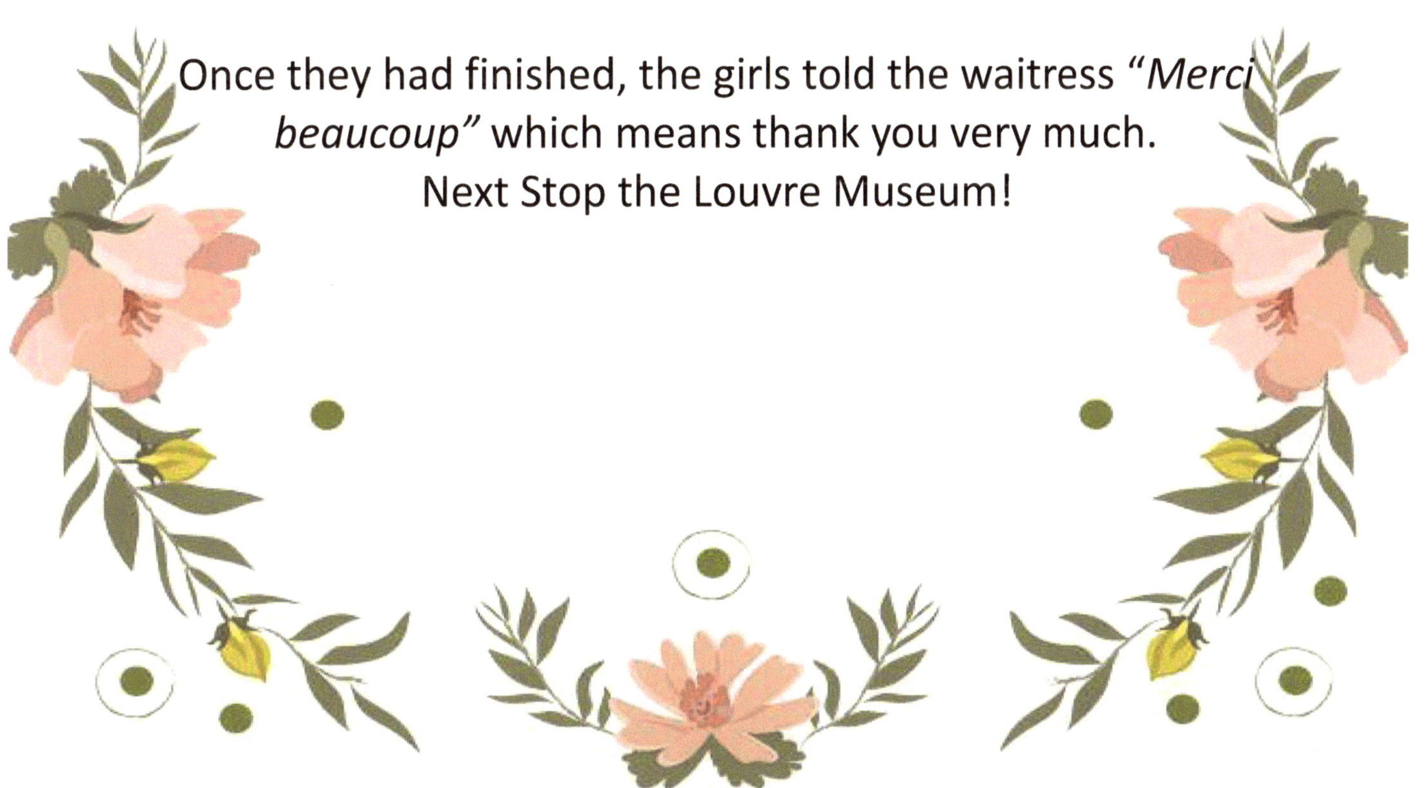

"The Louvre, or the Louvre Museum, is the world's largest art museum and a historic monument in Paris, France, and is best known for being the home of the Mona Lisa," explained Jazz.

"The Louvre still topped the list of most-visited art museums in the world in 2020.
The museum is housed in the Louvre Palace, originally built in the late 12th to 13th century under Philip II", Jazz continued.

"Wow it's beautiful." Or "Belle," in French that means beautiful." JoJo explained.

CAFE
Come in we are Open
CANDY SHOP
Sorry we are Closed

Next up the Montmartre Safari!
This unique village atmosphere of the bohemian district can teach us about
the famous international artists such as Picasso, Dali, and more!
The we can take the cable car and get the best view of the city, atop the Sacré-Coeur hill!
"This sounds perfect" exclaimed JoJo.

Sweet & Chocolate
Chocolate
FRUIT DROPS
HAND MADE
Chocolate
NATURAL DARK
Chocolate

Next stop is Sweet & Chocolate in Paris – Family Walking Tour!

"I love chocolate" Jazz shouted. A pastry and chocolate tour to delight the whole family, from the youngest to the eldest!

Did you know that there are at least 8 tastings to discover the best of French sweets: macarons, chocolate mousse, toffees?

We get to experience a thrilling walking tour full of riddles and anecdotes in the lovely Saint-Germain-des-Près neighborhood.

And don't forget that at the end of the tour, each member will be rewarded with the chocolate bar of their own design!

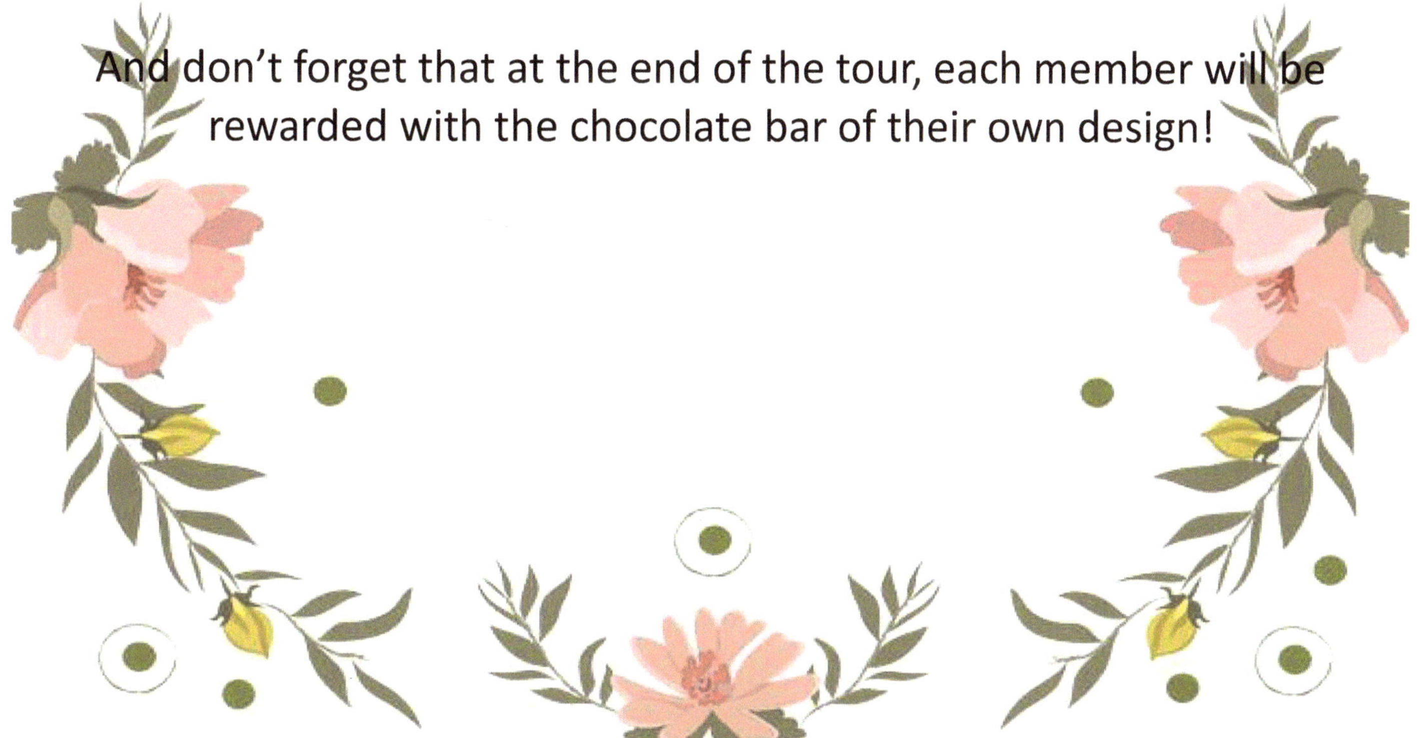

The next few stops were the Mystery at the Opera Garnier. We did the Paris Street Art Tour & Workshop and the History of Paris – Family Tour.

The last thing we enjoyed was the Paris Seine River Family Cruise Tour.

The girls admired Paris's main highlights on a luxury cruise on the legendary Seine River.
They even provided entertainment with an activity booklet and fun facts.

We had such a memorable and unique family experience, and we ended the night with a toast with the Eiffel Tower in the background.

Boggs Family

We had such a good time in Pairs. We hope you guys will join us again on our next big trip.

Au Revoir – The Most Common Way of Saying Goodbye in French. "Au revoir" means "until we see each other again."

 Join two adventurous sisters as they travel the world, learning new things. On this trip, they take in the sights, sounds, and tastes of Paris, France! Explore the city with them, visiting all the must-see landmarks in Paris. Jazz and JoJo are twins and best friends. They participate in the same clubs, enjoy the same foods, and are partners on all their school projects. Join them in their adventures to see all the wonderful places they travel all over the world. Let Jazz and JoJo be your tour guides through the beautiful city lights of Las Vegas, all the way to Paris France. Whether you're planning a trip to Paris or you want to visit the city through the pages of this book, you'll love joining the girls on their adventure. Don't forget your passport! TwinFabulous is perfect for children who are twins, and just as perfect for children who aren't!

 La'Tosha Price is a professional medical vendor consultant. She's a native of Bardstown, Kentucky, married to Carlos Price for twenty-one blissful years, and the proud mother of three daughters and one son. She's also a grandmother. La' Tosha has been honored with the Positive Leadership Award, the Dean's Award from Spencerian College, and the President's Club Award from Beta Sigma Chi Chapter. In her youth, she won a Young Leader Writing Award, had her story featured on the front page of the Bardstown newspaper, and received an honorary trip to South Carolina with co-writer Cabrina Logan of Bardstown Kentucky.

La' Tosha and husband Carlos are Assistant Pastors at Faith Convent Fellowship Church of Winter Park, FL under the direction of Bishop Barry Brandon. When La' Tosha is not working, she loves to write, swim, participate in theatrical arts, and go bike riding. She and her family reside in Kissimmee, Florida